This book belongs to:

- - - - - - - - - - - - - - - - - - - -

- - - - - - - - - - - - - - - - - - - -

Other magical books by Enid Blyton

The New Adventures of the Wishing-Chair:
The Island of Surprises
The New Adventures of the Wishing-Chair:
Spellworld

⭐✩⭐✩⭐

The Adventures of the Wishing-Chair
The Wishing-Chair Again
More Wishing-Chair Stories

⭐✩⭐✩⭐

The Enchanted Wood
The Magic Faraway Tree
The Folk of the Faraway Tree

⭐✩⭐✩⭐

The Enchanted World:
Silky and the Rainbow Feather
The Enchanted World:
Melody and the Enchanted Harp
The Enchanted World: Petal and the Eternal Bloom
The Enchanted World:
Pinx and the Ring of Midnight
The Enchanted World: Bizzy and the Bedtime Bear

Enid Blyton's
The NEW Adventures of the
Wishing-Chair

The Land of Mythical Creatures

Illustrated by Erica-Jane Waters

EGMONT

Special thanks to Narinder Dhami

EGMONT
We bring stories to life

The New Adventures of the Wishing-Chair:
The Land of Mythical Creatures
First published in Great Britain 2009
by Egmont UK Limited
239 Kensington High Street
London W8 6SA

Enid Blyton® Text and illustration copyright
© 2009 Chorion Rights Limited. All rights reserved.
Illustrations by Erica-Jane Waters

The moral rights of the author and illustrator have been asserted

ISBN 978 1 4052 4388 9

1 3 5 7 9 10 8 6 4 2

www.egmont.co.uk

A CIP catalogue record for this title is available
from the British Library

Printed and bound in Great Britain by Clay Ltd, St Ives plc

Contents

The Characters

Jack

Jessica

Toymaker

Wishler

The Ogre

Flick

Dolly

Buster

Miranda

'Hurrah!' Wishler shouted as he did

a little dance and waved his cleaning

cloth in the air. 'We're all done.'

'This looks great!' Jack leaned on

the broom handle and glanced around

the garden shed. He'd just finished

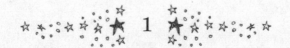

sweeping the floor and Wishler had done a great job cleaning the window. The shed looked very different from the dark, dusty place it had been before, especially because his sister, Jessica, had painted the walls bright blue yesterday.

Jack put the broom against the wall and dusted off his hands. 'What do you

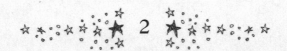 2

think of your new home, Wishler?'

'I'm going to *love* living here!' the pixie replied. He swept off his little green hat and bowed with a flourish.

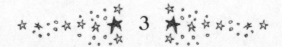

'As will the wishing-chair.'

The wooden wishing-chair, a gift from the magical Toymaker, stood in the middle of the shed, looking very much at home. Jack, Jessica and Wishler had polished it carefully and now the beautiful, colourful paintings that covered the chair glowed in the sunlight streaming through the window.

The door of the shed opened
and Wishler gave a squeak of fear
before ducking out of sight behind
a tall cupboard.
Jessica stepped
in with a
sketch pad
and pencil
in her hand.

Jack sighed with relief. 'I thought you might have been Mum or Dad.'

'Don't panic,' Jessica said. 'I made them promise to knock before they come in from now on. After all, this shed's our secret den.' She winked. 'Now, Wishler will always have time to hide!'

The pixie stepped out from behind

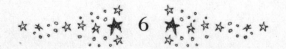

the cupboard and beamed at her. 'Great idea, Jessica.'

She smiled. 'You know, when we first moved to Noware, Jack and I were *really* bored. Then we found the wishing-chair, met you and started having adventures! You're our best friend Wishler and we want you to feel right at home.'

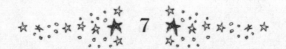

'Oh, I do!' the pixie assured her.

'What have you been up to, Jessica?' Jack asked, pointing at the sketch pad. 'You always manage to disappear when there's work to be done!'

Jessica grinned and poked her tongue out at him. 'I have to draw a horse for my art project,' she explained. 'I've been trying to sketch

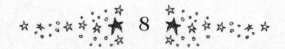

8

the horses in the field at the back of

the garden, but they won't come near

me. I'm never going to get it done!'

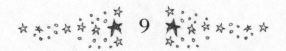

9

She heaved a huge sigh.

Jack could see that his sister looked worried.

Wishler shook his head. 'I think all this schoolwork has addled your brain, Jessica!'

She looked confused. '*What*?'

Wishler pointed at the wishing-chair. 'Remember what we said?

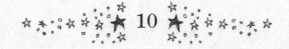

Now we've finished tidying the shed,

it's time for another adventure! I'll

take you to the Land of Mythical

Creatures to

see my friend

Miranda the

unicorn.'

   'Perfect!'

Jessica exclaimed.

'A unicorn is just like a horse, except it has a horn.'

Wishler nodded. 'And Miranda would be very happy for you to draw her.'

'Aren't unicorns kind of boring?' Jack asked grumpily. 'Like you said, Jess, they're just horses with horns.'

'Boring?' Wishler batted Jack's arm

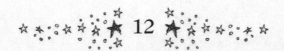

with his hat. 'Unicorns are wonderful, magical creatures. They can heal most illnesses just by touching the sick person or creature with their horn. Making creatures better is Miranda's job. And there are all kinds of other things to see in the Land of Mythical Creatures, like fierce trolls and fire-breathing dragons!'

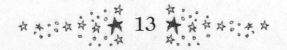

'Dragons,' Jack said, his voice low. He imagined the huge winged creatures soaring overhead. How amazing would it be to see one in real life? 'Let's go right away!'

The three of them sat down on the wishing-chair and rocked it three times. Bright blue sparks whizzed all around them.

'We wish to go to the Land of Mythical Creatures!' Jessica cried.

Chapter Two

There was a final flash of blue light, and a second later Jack, Jessica and Wishler felt the chair land with a gentle bump.

'Look at this place!' Jack said. They had come to rest on a lawn in the

middle of a town square. All around them were tall, thin buildings made of gold, silver and bronze. The metal shimmered in the sunlight.

'Everything is so pretty!' Jessica exclaimed taking in the leafy trees, laden with glittering silver apples that stood in the middle of the square.

'Look, the wishing-chair has

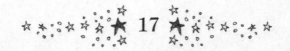

disguised itself again,' Wishler said.

Jack looked down and saw that the chair had changed into a long wooden bench, but was still covered with paintings.

Suddenly the clip-clop of hooves echoed loudly across the square.

'Is that Miranda?' Jessica asked, turning eagerly round.

'No, it's a centaur!' Jack cried, his eyes wide with amazement at the half-man, half-horse.

'He's not *quite* right for your art  project,' Wishler said with a smile, as the centaur trotted past. Jessica laughed.

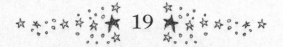

Jack spotted a strange-looking beast with the body of a lion and the head and wings of an eagle looking in a shop window. 'What kind of creature is that, Wishler?' Jack asked.

'That's a griffin,' Wishler explained. 'They can fly higher and faster than any other mythical creature. Oh, and they are the best comedians!'

 20

'Let's go and say hello to him,' Jessica said. 'I would love to hear one of his jokes.'

But Jack was frowning. 'Haven't you noticed how *miserable* everyone seems?' he said. 'Look at the griffin properly.'

Wishler and Jessica peered at the winged creature. He did indeed look

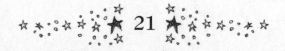

rather unhappy. He coughed loudly, and a cloud of yellow sparkles shot from his beak. Jack and Jessica watched in amazement as the mist of sparkles turned into a fox that bounded away.

'Is that normal?' asked Jack, as the griffin continued to cough up more sparkles that turned into animals.

Wishler shook his head, looking rather worried.

'Do you mind if I sit down?' asked a quavery voice beside them.

Jack and Jessica turned to see yet another magical creature. She had the body of a lion, but the head of a human.

It's a sphinx! Jack thought,

remembering the sphinx statues that he saw on holiday in Egypt.

'Yes, do please sit down,' Wishler replied politely.

The elderly sphinx carefully lowered herself on to the bench.

'I'm so glad there's a seat here now,' she said, rubbing at her arms. 'This strange illness makes me itch

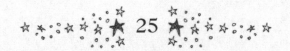

all over, I need to sit down and have a good scratch!' The sphinx purred in satisfaction as she attacked a really itchy part on her shoulder.

'Why is *everyone* here ill?' Jessica whispered to Wishler. 'Can't Miranda heal them with her magic?'

The pixie shrugged. 'I don't know what's going on.' He turned to the

sphinx. 'My dear lady, have you tried sitting in a bath full of cold copper coins? Isn't that the best cure for sphinx itches?'

'Oh my,' the sphinx said. 'What a brilliant suggestion!' And she dashed off before any of them could ask about the unicorn.

Jack looked around the market square at the unhappy villagers. 'Why isn't Miranda here, helping everyone?'

'I know what we'll do,' Wishler

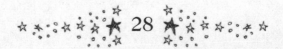

announced. 'Dolly, my third cousin on my mother's side, lives right here in the Land of Mythical Creatures. She'll be able to tell us *exactly* what's going on!'

Chapter
Three

Wishler led Jack and Jessica towards a tall, crooked house made of shining bronze that stood in the town square. As they approached, the delicious smell of baking bread wafted towards them through an open window.

'This is the bakery,' Wishler explained. 'Dolly lives just above it.'

Jack and Jessica peeped into the bakery. To their amazement, they saw three little elves dancing a jig on a big mound of dough on the floor. As they watched, the elves collided into each other. Two landed on their bottoms, and one landed head-first

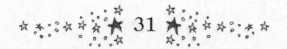

in the dough.

'What *are* they doing?' Jessica asked.

'It's strange, isn't it?' Wishler shook his head in bewilderment. 'Elf bread

is the best bread in the world because the elves knead the dough by dancing on it with their toes, but these chaps can't dance at all!'

'Maybe they're ill too,' Jack guessed, as Wishler rang the bell of his cousin's house.

They heard footsteps coming downstairs and the sound of loud

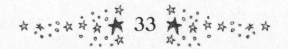

sniffling. The door opened, and there stood a round-faced, pointy-eared little pixie, wearing a bright red dress and snow-white apron. But, unlike Wishler, she was green all over.

'Wishler!' she exclaimed. 'It's been ages.'

'Hello, Dolly,' said Wishler, giving the other pixie a hug. 'These are my

friends, Jack and Jessica.' He paused. 'Are you OK, Dolly? You look awfully green!'

'It's a long story,' Dolly explained, still sniffing loudly. 'Come in, and I'll tell you all about it.'

They went inside and Dolly led them up a twisting, bronze staircase.

'Now, what's happened?' asked

Wishler, as they sat down in Dolly's pretty little living-room.

'Dear Wishler, I'm ill, and so is everyone else in town.' Dolly sniffled sadly. 'That wretched young wizard, Flick, came to visit and sold everyone these delicious chocolates. Now we're all unwell.'

'Flick the wizard!' Jack exclaimed, glancing at Jessica. 'We know him.'

'Yes, he gave us an invisibility spell.' Jessica sighed. 'Only it didn't work and we got chased by a giant, cross teddy-bear.'

'Yes, that Flick is a very naughty wizard,' Dolly said.

'But where's Miranda?' asked Wishler.

'Yesterday Miranda went to visit the scary ogre who lives in a cave deep in the forest,' Dolly explained. 'He was really sick, so Miranda went to heal

him first. But she hasn't come back.'

Dolly shuddered. 'We think the ogre

has *eaten* her!'

'Poor Miranda!' Jessica said in

dismay.

'Ogres are awfully mean creatures,'

Dolly explained.

Suddenly, they all heard a loud,

booming sound, and the house began

to shake. There were shouts of alarm from outside.

'It's him,' Dolly cried fearfully. 'He's eaten Miranda and now he wants to gobble down someone else!'

Jack and Jessica rushed to the window. There, stomping across the square, was a huge, angry ogre!

Chapter
Four

'He's enormous!' Jessica whispered.

Her brother nodded, his eyes wide.

The ogre was so big, he was almost

as high as Dolly's first-floor window.

As he strode through the square,

Jessica saw the townsfolk run for

cover, diving behind trees and inside houses.

'He's frightening all the sick creatures,' Jack said as the ogre let out a raspy roar. 'We have to do something, Jessica!'

Jessica nodded. She and her brother poked their heads out of the window. It was only just big enough for the

two of them. 'Where's Miranda?' she

demanded in a loud voice.

The ogre stopped, turned his

massive head and stared at Jessica,

baring his big yellow teeth. Jessica's legs felt like jelly, but she stared straight back at him.

'Urrgh!' the ogre said in a very hoarse voice. Then he shook his head, pointing at his throat.

'Oh! I think he has a bad sore throat,' Jessica guessed. 'That's why he can't talk.'

'Why don't you act out what happened to Miranda?' Jack yelled up at the ogre. 'Like charades!'

The ogre put his hands on top of his head in the shape of a horn.

'Unicorn?' Jessica questioned.

The ogre nodded. Then, to Jessica's dismay, he rubbed his tummy. 'Oh no!' she said. 'He really has eaten

Miranda!' There were gasps of horror from all the townspeople in the square.

The ogre shook his head. He swallowed a couple of times and then managed to croak just one word.

'Hungry!'

'Thank goodness, he hasn't eaten Miranda *yet*,' Wishler said joyfully

from behind them.

'But I think he will soon,' Jack said. 'He must have trapped her in his cave.'

'You're a very bad ogre,' shouted one of the centaurs in the square below. 'Bring back Miranda and leave us alone!'

'Yes, we want Miranda back!' the

other creatures chorused.

Jack and Jessica watched as an elf hurled a custard pie at the ogre, and then hid. The

ogre stamped

his foot in

rage, setting

everything

shaking. Behind

them, Dolly gave a little moan. Jack glanced round and saw that the little pixie had fainted with fear, but luckily Wishler caught her as she fell.

Jessica couldn't help feeling a bit sorry for the ogre as the creatures yelled up at him. But even if he *was* hungry, he shouldn't be threatening to eat the magical unicorn who came

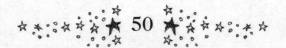

to help him!

The ogre turned back to Jessica and Jack and began making lots of complicated signs with his hands, pointing up and then down but neither of them could figure out what he was trying to tell them.

'Look, if you just bring Miranda back right now, everyone will stop

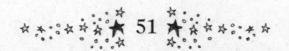 51

being horrible to you,' Jack told him

firmly.

The ogre's face darkened and he shook his head. Then he tore a huge branch off one of the silver apple trees, and, brandishing it threateningly, he stomped off.

'We've got to save Miranda,' said Jessica, as she and her brother turned away from the window. 'The Toymaker gave us the wishing-chair so that we

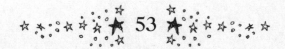

could help those in trouble.'

Wishler and Jack nodded.

'But *how*?' her brother asked.

Chapter
Five

'Dolly!' called a voice from the window. 'I heard you scream. Are you all right?'

Jack and Jessica turned and saw a dragon with shiny green scales hovering outside. He was bigger than

the tallest apple tree and little puffs

of smoke curled from his nostrils.

'Wow,' Jack whispered.

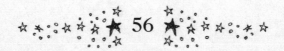

'Oh, I'm fine now, thank you, Buster,' called Dolly weakly. Wishler helped her to an armchair. 'But isn't it terrible about Miranda? That ogre has kidnapped her and he's going to eat her!'

'It's awful,' the dragon agreed.

'You remember my cousin Wishler, don't you?' Dolly went on. 'These are

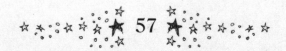

his friends, Jack and Jessica.'

'Pleased to meet you.' Buster nodded his scaly head politely. His silvery-grey eyes twinkled.

'H-Hello, Buster,' Jack stuttered out. Jessica managed to give a little wave.

The dragon let out a sneeze and flames flickered from his nostrils and

set the window-box of marigolds on

fire. Dolly gave a cry of dismay.

'Leave this to me!' Wishler said

quickly. He closed

his eyes and

muttered

a few words,

and then

snapped his fingers.

To Jack and Jessica's amazement, a tiny, black rain-cloud appeared just above the window-box and began to rain down on the fire. The flames were put out instantly.

'Wishler, you never told us you could do magic!' Jessica exclaimed.

'Well, I'm very, *very* rusty because I was trapped in the wishing-chair

for so long,' the pixie replied, looking rather pleased with himself. 'But it seems to be coming back to me bit by bit.'

'Sorry about the marigolds,' Buster said. 'I just can't shake this cold that Flick's chocolates gave me. I wish Miranda was here.'

'We're going to rescue her,' said

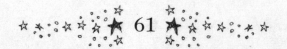

Jack. 'But we need to get to the ogre's cave in the forest before he does.'

'I could take you,' offered Buster.

'Are you sure you're well enough?' Jessica asked.

The dragon nodded. 'Even though I'm sick, I'm sure I can fly faster than the ogre can walk.'

'Let's go right away,' Wishler said.

'Oh, do be careful!' Dolly called anxiously as Jack, Jessica and Wishler ran downstairs, calling their goodbyes.

Buster was waiting in the town square, his emerald scales glinting in the sunshine. Jack, Jessica and Wishler climbed on to his back. The dragon's scales were cool and rough.

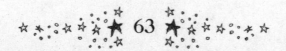

Jack sat at the front with Jessica and
Wishler behind him, and they all held
on to each other.

'Let's go, Buster!' Jack yelled.

The dragon began to flap his huge wings. Jack and Jessica felt a rush of air as Buster rose up from the ground and began to climb high into the sky above the twinkling metal houses.

Suddenly Jack heard Buster sniffing and spluttering a little. 'Buster, are you OK?' he asked.

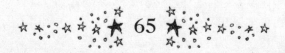

'No, I don't think I am. Hold on!'
The dragon let out a huge sneeze and
a ball of fire burst from his nostrils.
Instantly Buster plummeted down
towards the ground, taking Jack,
Jessica and Wishler with him.

Chapter Six

'Stop!' Wishler shouted.

Jessica gripped on to her brother. She could feel him shaking with fear.

'You've got to straighten up, Buster,' Jessica yelled.

The ground was racing towards

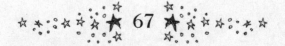

them but at the last possible moment they soared upwards again. Wishler, Jack and Jessica heaved sighs of relief.

'Sorry for the bumpy ride,' Buster called over his shoulder. 'Sneezing completely disrupts my flying technique.'

'I think I've turned as green as

poor Dolly!' Wishler whispered in Jessica's ear.

Soon they'd left the town behind and were flying over lush green countryside. They saw a sparkling lake where mermaids sat basking in the sun, and then they saw a large forest ahead of them.

'This is where the ogre lives,'

Buster explained. He flew over the forest and circled in the air, pointing to the entrance of a huge cave with his claw. 'I can't land too close to the trees in case I set them on fire with my sneezes! But I'll take you to a clearing not far away.'

'Hurry, Buster,' Jessica said urgently. 'We *must* get to the cave before the ogre and rescue Miranda!'

The dragon flew on a short distance.

Then he floated down from the sky

and landed in a clearing in the forest.

He let out another little sneeze as he

came to rest,

scorching a

small patch

of grass.

'I'll wait here for you,' Buster said as Jack, Jessica and Wishler climbed off his back. 'I feel quite ill, so I better have a bit of a rest.'

'Thanks, Buster,' said Jack.

The three friends ran off through the forest, past a deep, rocky chasm and towards the ogre's cave.

When they reached it, Jack

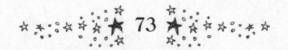

slowly looked inside.

'I can't see or hear the ogre,' he said in a low voice. 'We beat him back! Let's search for Miranda.'

Jack, Jessica and Wishler crept inside the cave. It was very dark and gloomy and the only light came from a fire in the middle of it.

A noise from the back of the cave

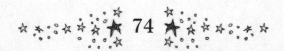

caught Jessica's attention. 'That might be Miranda,' she whispered. 'Come on!'

They stepped deeper into the cave. It wound away to the left and Jack realised that it was much bigger than it looked from the outside.

Jessica could hear heavy breathing ahead of them. Peering around the corner, she saw the ogre standing at a table, his back to them.

'Time for yum, yum,' he whispered in a very hoarse voice.

Jessica's heart sank. 'He's about to eat Miranda.'

'Oi you, stop!' Jack yelled, rushing into full view.

The ogre spun round in surprise,

and a pink-frosted fairy cake dropped

from his hand on to the ground.

Jack was confused. 'Where's Miranda?' he asked, staring at the fairy cake.

The ogre let out a roar. The three friends backed away.

'He must have eaten Miranda already and now he's having dessert!' Wishler sobbed.

'We've made him *really* mad now,'

Jessica shouted. 'Run for it!'

Chapter
Seven

Wishler, Jack and Jessica dashed
out of the cave. They could feel the
ground shaking under their feet as
the ogre chased after them.

'Which way did we come?' Wishler
gasped, his face white. 'I can't

remember! Help!'

'Quick, let's go this way!' Jessica yelled.

But only a few steps away from the cave, Jack gave a shout and grabbed Jessica's arm. 'Careful!'

Jessica skidded to a halt at the edge of a deep, rocky ravine. One more step and she would have tumbled

down into the depths.

The ogre was still coming after them, but there was no way of getting across to the other side.

'We're trapped!' Wishler moaned.

The ogre came charging towards them but stopped just in front of the three friends. He dropped to his knees and peered over the edge of the ravine. Then he grunted at them and pointed over the edge. Jessica looked at his face. His hairy brow was furrowed with concern.

'He's not trying to eat us,' said Jessica. 'He's telling us something.'

The ogre nodded and pointed downwards again. Jack, Jessica and Wishler shuffled cautiously to the

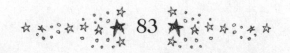

edge of the chasm and looked into it.

To her amazement, Jessica saw a beautiful white unicorn lying on a ledge far below her.

'Miranda,' Wishler cried. 'You're alive!'

'Hello, Wishler, my friend,' Miranda called, lifting her sleek head. Her golden horn gleamed in the

sunlight. 'I'm so glad to see you! I

came here to cure Grumble the ogre,

but on my way to his cave, I slipped

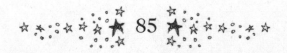

and fell. He has been trying to help me.'

'So that's why Grumble came to the village,' Jessica said. 'But no one listened.'

Jack spotted a branch next to Miranda, still with a few silver apples left on it. 'That's the branch he took from the tree in the square,' Jack

pointed out. 'I think I understand now, when he came to town he was trying to tell us that *Miranda* was hungry – not himself!'

'Yes, Grumble's been doing his very best to feed me,' Miranda explained.

Jessica turned to the ogre. 'Grumble, you're not a mean ogre at all!' she declared. 'You're very kind.'

Jack nodded in agreement.

Grumble blushed, looking pleased.

'I'm sorry, Grumble,' Wishler said.
'I shouldn't have assumed that you
were bad. I should have
given you a chance.'
The little pixie went
and gave the ogre's
foot a hug.

'But how are we going to get Miranda out?' asked Jessica.

Jack glanced at the forest around them, looking for an inspiration. Suddenly he noticed some long vines hanging from a tree. They looked like thick, leafy ropes.

'Hey, maybe we could use vines to pull Miranda out of the chasm,' Jack

suggested. 'I bet Grumble's strong enough.'

The ogre nodded eagerly.

Jack, Jessica and Wishler ran to the tree and pulled down the three sturdiest vines. Then they made loops in the end of them.

'One of us will have to climb down and tie the ropes around Miranda,'

said Jessica, looking worried.

'I'll go,' Jack offered. 'I've done rock-climbing on school trips.'

Wishler, Jessica and Grumble watched anxiously as Jack lowered himself over the edge of the chasm.

'Be careful!' Miranda called from below.

Jack tried not to look down as he

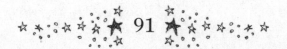

searched for toeholds and handholds

in the rocky surface. The wind

whistled past his ears and his heart

was racing as he moved slowly down towards Miranda.

It seemed to take hours, but at last Jack felt the narrow ledge under his feet.

'You're a very brave boy,' said Miranda, nuzzling Jack's shoulder.

Grumble threw the looped ends of the vines down to Jack. Quickly

he wrapped them around Miranda's smooth, snow-white middle. Then he climbed on to the unicorn's back and looked up at Jessica, Wishler and the ogre. 'We're ready.'

'Pull, Grumble!' Jessica called.

Grumble began to haul on the vines. Jack clung on to the unicorn's silky mane as he and Miranda were

lifted up into the air. Glancing down into the chasm below, Jack gulped. It was *very* deep.

All of a sudden there was a loud tearing noise.

Jack looked up and saw one of the vines splitting under their weight. 'It's tearing!' he yelled.

Chapter
Eight

'Stop pulling, Grumble!' Jessica shouted and peered down over the edge.

The vine split a little more, and Jack's heart thumped as they dropped down a bit. 'It's not going to hold

much longer,' he yelled.

'I've got it!' Wishler shouted.
'Miranda, you can heal the vine with
your horn!'

The unicorn immediately touched
her horn to the vine and a golden
light surrounded it. Jack watched in
amazement as the vine knitted itself
back together, looking even thicker

than before. Quickly Miranda touched the other two vines as well.

'Just in case!' she said to Jack.

Jack gripped Miranda's mane as Grumble pulled the two of them upwards. A few moments later they reached the top of the chasm and Wishler and Jessica pulled them from the edge.

'Thank you!' Miranda said gratefully. She touched Grumble's throat with her horn, and briefly he was bathed in a soft golden light.

Looking delighted, the ogre cleared his throat.

'Oh, I'm cured!' he exclaimed. 'Thank you, Miranda. Will you all come and have some tea?' He looked sad for a moment. 'I don't get many visitors.'

'We'd love to, Grumble,' Jack replied immediately.

'I mustn't be too long though,' Miranda added. 'I have sick villagers to heal.'

Grumble led the way back to his cave where he served up tea and frosted fairy cakes.

'These are great!' Jack said, taking a second helping.

'I love cooking,' Grumble explained shyly. 'I'm sorry for roaring at you earlier. I had just finished icing that fairy cake I dropped.'

'That's OK, Grumble,' Jack said.

'Have another fairy cake, Wishler,' said Jessica, holding out the plate. But as she did so, the pixie suddenly flickered in and out of focus.

'Uh oh,' Jessica said. 'That means we have to go.' She jumped to her feet. 'The wishing-chair is getting restless and it might leave without us.'

'Come again soon,' Grumble called, waving from the cave entrance as Miranda, Jack, Jessica and Wishler hurried away, taking a fairy cake for Buster the dragon.

'We will,' Jack called back, 'and we'll tell the townspeople what a nice ogre you are!'

'Oh, I just remembered,' Jessica exclaimed, as they returned to the clearing where Buster was snoring loudly. 'I came here to draw Miranda for my art project, and now I won't have time.'

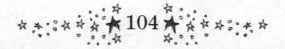

Jessica explained to the unicorn how she'd had no luck trying to draw the horses in the field back home.

'Just offer them an apple and they'll come to you,' Miranda told her. 'Horses love apples!'

She touched her horn to Buster's head, and the dragon sleepily opened his eyes.

'Oh, I had a lovely dream that Miranda came and cured me,' Buster sighed. His eyes widened as he saw the unicorn.

'Yes, it's really me, Buster.' Miranda laughed. 'Now, I must get back to the town and heal everyone else.'

After giving him his fairy cake, Jack, Jessica and Wishler jumped on to Buster's back and the dragon soared up into the sky. This time their flight was much smoother and trouble-free. Miranda galloped along below them.

She was moving so fast she looked just like a white blur.

Buster came to land in the town square, and everyone was cheering with excitement as they spotted Miranda cantering towards them.

'Miranda's back,' they cried. 'She's safe!'

The townsfolk crowded around the

unicorn and Miranda touched her horn to each and every one of them.

'Well done, all of you,' said Dolly, rushing over to Wishler, Jessica and Jack. Miranda had cured her and she wasn't green any more. 'You saved Miranda from that mean ogre.'

'Grumble *isn't* mean!' Jessica announced, standing up on Buster's

back so that everyone could hear her.

'He was just trying to help Miranda.'

She quickly explained what had

happened, and everyone looked a

little ashamed.

'I shall bake Grumble some fairy

cakes and invite him to tea,' Dolly

declared, and the other creatures

nodded in agreement.

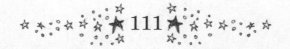

'Wishler's flickering again,' Jack said to Jessica. 'We have to go.'

Wishler, Jack and Jessica said goodbye to their new friends and, giving Miranda, Dolly and Buster a hug each, they ran back to the wishing-chair.

'It hasn't undisguised itself yet,' Jack said, looking at the bench, 'so

we're just in time.'

'Show yourself!' Wishler said, tapping the chair three times.

Instantly the bench turned back into the wishing-chair and they all climbed on to it.

'Home!' Jack shouted.

Bright blue sparks shot out from the chair's rockers and fizzed around

them. A few seconds later they were all back in the shed at the bottom of the garden.

'That adventure was so much fun,' Jack announced, jumping off the chair.

'And useful too.' Jessica headed for the door. 'I'm off to get some apples for

the horses, so I can draw them.'

'I can't wait for our next adventure,' Wishler said.

'Me neither,' Jessica replied, 'but first I've got an art project to finish!'

EGMONT PRESS: ETHICAL PUBLISHING

Egmont Press is about turning writers into successful authors and children into passionate readers – producing books that enrich and entertain. As a responsible children's publisher, we go even further, considering the world in which our consumers are growing up.

Safety First
Naturally, all of our books meet legal safety requirements. But we go further than this; every book with play value is tested to the highest standards – if it fails, it's back to the drawing-board.

Made Fairly
We are working to ensure that the workers involved in our supply chain – the people that make our books – are treated with fairness and respect.

Responsible Forestry
We are committed to ensuring all our papers come from environmentally and socially responsible forest sources.

**For more information, please visit our website at
www.egmont.co.uk/ethical**

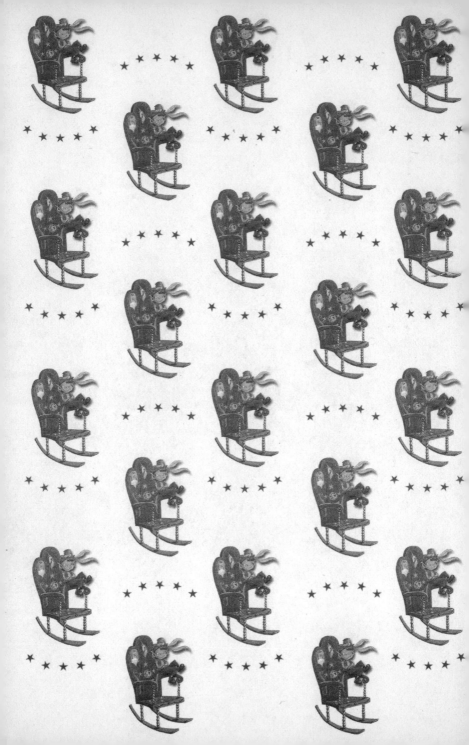